ESPECIALLY FOR

THE POLAR EXPRESS

Written and Illustrated by

CHRIS VAN ALLSBURG

CLARION BOOKS

An Imprint of HarperCollinsPublishers

BOSTON   NEW YORK

BONUS
A downloadable recording of the story read by
the renowned actor Liam Neeson can be accessed at
hc.com/freedownloads.
Access code: RING

To Karen

Library of Congress Cataloging-in-Publication Data

Van Allsburg, Chris.
   The Polar Express.

   Summary: A magical train ride on Christmas Eve takes a boy
to the North Pole to receive a special gift from Santa Claus.
   [1. North Pole—Fiction.   2. Santa Claus—Fiction.
3. Christmas—Fiction.]   I. Title.
P27.V266Po   1985   {E}   85-10907
ISBN 978-0-544-58014-5

Library of Congress Catalog Card Number: 85-10907

Printed in China

23 SCP 20 19 18 17

THE POLAR EXPRESS

On Christmas Eve, many years ago, I lay quietly in my bed. I did not rustle the sheets. I breathed slowly and silently. I was listening for a sound—a sound a friend had told me I'd never hear—the ringing bells of Santa's sleigh.

"There is no Santa," my friend had insisted, but I knew he was wrong.

Late that night I did hear sounds, though not of ringing bells. From outside came the sounds of hissing steam and squeaking metal. I looked through my window and saw a train standing perfectly still in front of my house.

It was wrapped in an apron of steam. Snowflakes fell lightly around it. A conductor stood at the open door of one of the cars. He took a large pocket watch from his vest, then looked up at my window. I put on my slippers and robe. I tiptoed downstairs and out the door.

"All aboard," the conductor cried out. I ran up to him.

"Well," he said, "are you coming?"

"Where?" I asked.

"Why, to the North Pole of course," was his answer. "This is the Polar Express." I took his outstretched hand and he pulled me aboard.

The train was filled with other children, all in their pajamas and nightgowns. We sang Christmas carols and ate candies with nougat centers as white as snow. We drank hot cocoa as thick and rich as melted chocolate bars. Outside, the lights of towns and villages flickered in the distance as the Polar Express raced northward.

Soon there were no more lights to be seen. We traveled through cold, dark forests, where lean wolves roamed and white-tailed rabbits hid from our train as it thundered through the quiet wilderness.

We climbed mountains so high it seemed as if we would scrape the moon. But the Polar Express never slowed down. Faster and faster we ran along, rolling over peaks and through valleys like a car on a roller coaster.

The mountains turned into hills, the hills to snow-covered plains. We crossed a barren desert of ice—the Great Polar Ice Cap. Lights appeared in the distance. They looked like the lights of a strange ocean liner sailing on a frozen sea. "There," said the conductor, "is the North Pole."

The North Pole. It was a huge city standing alone at the top of the world, filled with factories where every Christmas toy was made.

At first we saw no elves.

"They are gathering at the center of the city," the conductor told us. "That is where Santa will give the first gift of Christmas."

"Who receives the first gift?" we all asked.

The conductor answered, "He will choose one of you."

"Look," shouted one of the children, "the elves." Outside we saw hundreds of elves. As our train drew closer to the center of the North Pole, we slowed to a crawl, so crowded were the streets with Santa's helpers. When the Polar Express could go no farther, we stopped and the conductor led us outside.

We pressed through the crowd to the edge of a large, open circle. In front of us stood Santa's sleigh. The reindeer were excited. They pranced and paced, ringing the silver sleigh bells that hung from their harnesses. It was a magical sound, like nothing I'd ever heard. Across the circle, the elves moved apart and Santa Claus appeared. The elves cheered wildly.

He marched over to us and, pointing to me, said, "Let's have this fellow here." He jumped into his sleigh. The conductor handed me up. I sat on Santa's knee and he asked, "Now, what would you like for Christmas?"

I knew that I could have any gift I could imagine. But the thing I wanted most for Christmas was not inside Santa's giant bag. What I wanted more than anything was one silver bell from Santa's sleigh. When I asked, Santa smiled. Then he gave me a hug and told an elf to cut a bell from a reindeer's harness. The elf tossed it up to Santa. He stood, holding the bell high above him, and called out, "The first gift of Christmas!"

A clock struck midnight as
the elves roared their approval.
Santa handed the bell to me,
and I put it in my bathrobe
pocket. The conductor helped
me down from the sleigh. Santa
shouted out the reindeer's
names and cracked his whip.
His team charged forward and
climbed into the air. Santa
circled once above us, then
disappeared in the cold, dark
polar sky.

As soon as we were back inside the Polar Express, the other children asked to see the bell. I reached into my pocket, but the only thing I felt was a hole. I had lost the silver bell from Santa Claus's sleigh. "Let's hurry outside and look for it," one of the children said. But the train gave a sudden lurch and started moving. We were on our way home.

It broke my heart to lose
the bell. When the train
reached my house, I sadly left
the other children. I stood
at my doorway and waved
good-bye. The conductor
said something from the
moving train, but I couldn't
hear him. "What?" I yelled
out.

He cupped his hands
around his mouth. "MERRY
CHRISTMAS," he shouted.
The Polar Express let out a
loud blast from its whistle
and sped away.

On Christmas morning my little sister Sarah and I opened our presents. When it looked as if everything had been unwrapped, Sarah found one last small box behind the tree. It had my name on it. Inside was the silver bell! There was a note: "Found this on the seat of my sleigh. Fix that hole in your pocket." Signed, "Mr. C."

I shook the bell. It made the most beautiful sound my sister and I had ever heard.

But my mother said, "Oh, that's too bad."

"Yes," said my father, "it's broken."

When I'd shaken the bell, my parents had not heard a sound.

At one time most of my friends could hear the bell, but as years passed, it fell silent for all of them. Even Sarah found one Christmas that she could no longer hear its sweet sound. Though I've grown old, the bell still rings for me as it does for all who truly believe.